# THE WISE WOMAN
# AND HER SECRET

# THE WISE WOMAN AND HER SECRET

by Eve Merriam
illustrated by Linda Graves

Simon & Schuster Books for Young Readers
Published by Simon & Schuster
New York • London • Toronto • Sydney • Tokyo • Singapore

Reprinted by arrangement with Simon & Schuster *Books for Young Readers*, a Division of Simon & Schuster Inc., for Silver Burdett Ginn Inc.

SIMON &SCHUSTER BOOKS FOR YOUNG READERS
Simon & Schuster Building, Rockefeller Center
1230 Avenue of the Americas, New York, New York 10020

Manufactured in Mexico.    2  3  4  5  6  7  8  9  10   RRD  98  97  96  95  94  93

Designed by Lucille Chomowicz.
The text of this book is set in Galliard.
The illustrations were done in pastel, colored pencil, water color and sepia ink.

Library of Congress Cataloging-in-Publication Data
Merriam, Eve. The wise woman and her secret. Summary: Although many try to force from the wise woman the secret of her wisdom, the truth is made clear only to a young girl who shows the capacity for wandering and wondering.  [1. Wisdom—Fiction.]  I. Graves, Linda, ill. II. Title. PZ7.M543Wj 1991  [E]—dc20   90-42406  ISBN 0-663-56231-7

For my beloved sister Helen—EM

For Stephen, Jeremiah, and Marshall—LG

Once, not so long ago, in the hills past the hollow, there lived a wise woman. She had long, dark hair that was streaked with white like patches of snow on the muddy spring ground. Her eyes were bright as blackberries, and she had a smile for every creature. Her voice was soft as the fur of her cat, yet you could hear her every word from far away.

She was so wise that people from many towns in the valley gathered together and came to seek her out. If they could discover the secret of her wisdom, how fortunate they might all become!

So they climbed and they clambered up the long, meandering path to where the wise woman lived. They all hurried as fast as possible. The quicker they got there, the sooner they would possess the secret of wisdom.

Only a little girl named Jenny fell behind. She kept picking up pebbles along the path, tossing them into the air, and trying to see if she could catch them.

"Don't lag, don't loiter, don't dawdle," people scolded, and pulled her along.

Faster and farther they journeyed, past orchards and silos, past walls and fences, until they came to an open field with a barn, a well, and a small wooden house.

The wise woman was sitting on the porch, rocking to the rhythm of a silent tune.

The tallest among the travelers pushed forward. "We are here for your secret. We have come a long distance, and we wish to get back home before dark, so give it to us without delay."

The tall man's wife tugged at his sleeve. "Say *please*," she whispered.

"'Please' is a pleasing word," the wise woman said, smiling, "but it can't make me give you the secret. You will have to discover it for yourselves. Please feel free to look all around you." And she would say no more, but kept on with her rocking.

So they went searching.

They ran to the barn, stamped on the earthen floor, jabbed at the piles of hay, pointed up at the rafters. Perhaps the secret was there.

The tall man lifted Jenny onto his shoulders; she could fetch it down for them.

"Oh!" Jenny exclaimed from her lofty perch, and, "Oh!" again.

She must have found it!

The tall man swung her down and held out his hand. But all Jenny had was a speckled feather and a twig in the shape of a Y with a silky cobweb spun inside.

So they went searching some more.

They tiptoed around the house, inspected the herbs in the window boxes, followed where the wise woman's cat went.

The cat led them to an old, gnarled blackthorn tree. They pulled quickly at the branches and winced as they drew back in pain.

Some began muttering. "There may be bad luck here."

"Yes," others said, nodding, "something strange going on. Perhaps this wise woman is a mischief-maker."

A graybeard stroked his chin. "She may not be of our kind at all. Perhaps she isn't a human being like us; perhaps she is from another planet."

"Yes, yes," they began to whisper in excitement, "that must be the answer. That is why we can't find the secret."

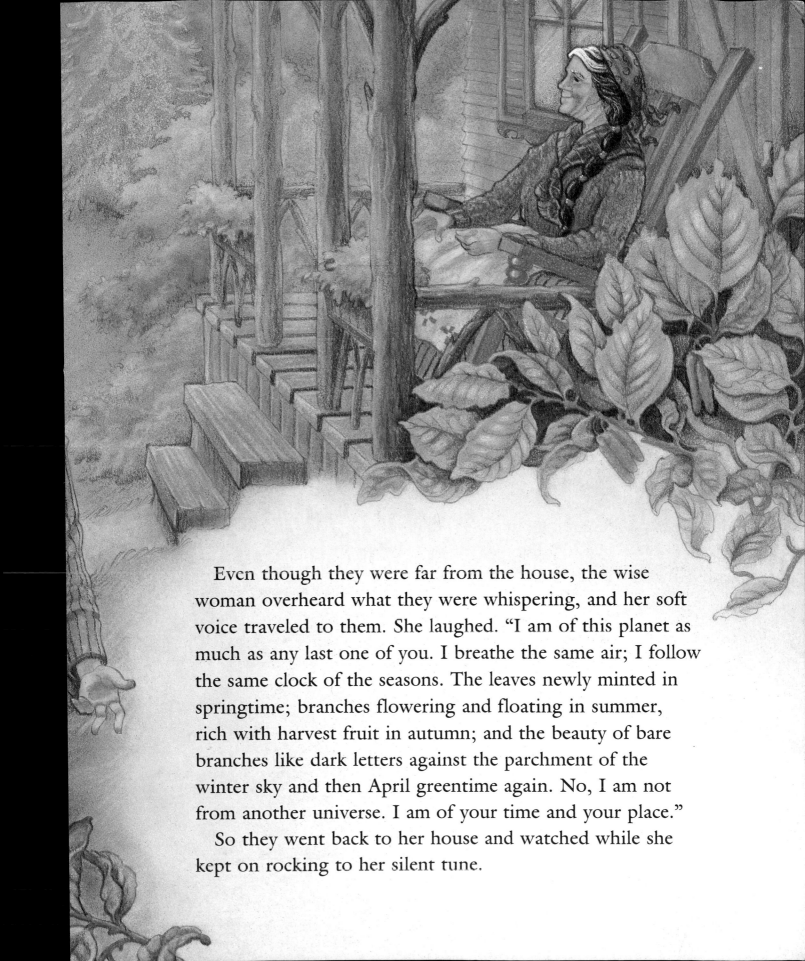

Even though they were far from the house, the wise woman overheard what they were whispering, and her soft voice traveled to them. She laughed. "I am of this planet as much as any last one of you. I breathe the same air; I follow the same clock of the seasons. The leaves newly minted in springtime; branches flowering and floating in summer, rich with harvest fruit in autumn; and the beauty of bare branches like dark letters against the parchment of the winter sky and then April greentime again. No, I am not from another universe. I am of your time and your place."

So they went back to her house and watched while she kept on rocking to her silent tune.

After a while, she got up and went to the well, filled a
bucket with water, and walked slowly back to the house.

They all watched, and as soon as she was out of sight,
they pounced. The secret must be at the bottom of the well!

Everyone crowded around while the strongest among
them brought up bucket after bucket.

Quicker, quicker, hoist the rope!

What a disappointment. Nothing after all but clear well water and a green, tarnished penny that someone must have thrown into the well ages ago for good luck.

"Surely wisdom is worth more than a penny," the strongest person grumbled, and threw the coin onto the ground.

Jenny looked at the drops of water glinting on the coin like dew in the early morning. As she looked, the green, tarnished metal seemed almost to melt into the green of the grass.

She picked up the coin and put it in her pocket.

Off everyone trooped—all except Jenny, who jumped up and down so she could hear the coin jingling against the pebbles in her pocket. She walked through the field and up to the porch of the house.

The wise woman was there, and as she rocked, Jenny nodded her head in rhythm. The wise woman changed to another silent tune and asked, "What do you have in your pocket, little girl?"

"Would you like to see?" Jenny offered.

"May I?" The wise woman invited Jenny to step closer.

Jenny handed over the coin, and the wise woman held it up to her eyes, peering closely. Then she turned it over and peered at the other side, then flipped it back again and spun it around and around in her hand. She threw it into the air, caught it, and made a tight fist.

"Shall I give it back to you?"

"Would you like to keep it?" Jenny asked.

"My dear child, it belongs to you." The wise woman opened her hand and held the coin out to Jenny.

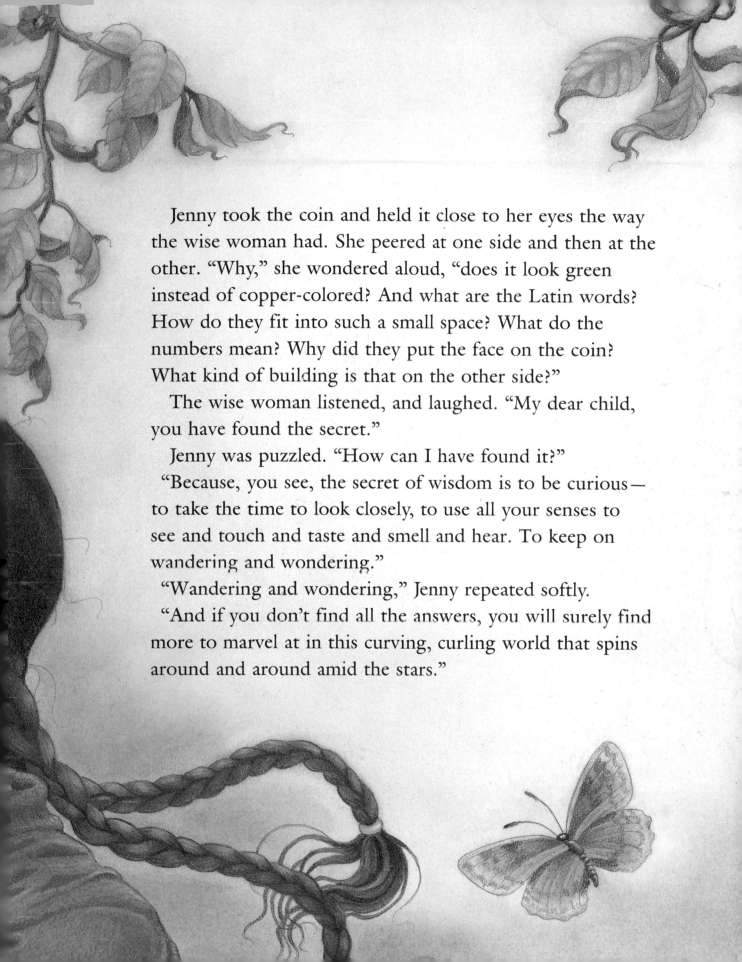

Jenny took the coin and held it close to her eyes the way the wise woman had. She peered at one side and then at the other. "Why," she wondered aloud, "does it look green instead of copper-colored? And what are the Latin words? How do they fit into such a small space? What do the numbers mean? Why did they put the face on the coin? What kind of building is that on the other side?"

The wise woman listened, and laughed. "My dear child, you have found the secret."

Jenny was puzzled. "How can I have found it?"

"Because, you see, the secret of wisdom is to be curious— to take the time to look closely, to use all your senses to see and touch and taste and smell and hear. To keep on wandering and wondering."

"Wandering and wondering," Jenny repeated softly.

"And if you don't find all the answers, you will surely find more to marvel at in this curving, curling world that spins around and around amid the stars."

Jenny heeded the wise woman's words. She returned home in good time, and she sauntered and sang, tasted and touched, and listened and laughed and cried; and she grew up to become a wise woman herself.